Enid Blyton

BRER BEAR'S RED CARROTS
CARROTS
and other stories

Enid Blyton

BRER BEAR'S RED CARROTS

and other stories

Illustrated by Teresa O'Brien

Purnell

Editor: Luigi Bonomi
Designer: Sonja Ferrier
Production: Garry Lewis

A Purnell Book
Text Copyright © 1950 Darrell Waters Ltd
Illustrations Copyright © 1987 Macdonald & Co (Publishers) Ltd
First published in this edition 1987 by
Macdonald & Co (Publishers) Ltd
Greater London House
Hampstead Road
London NW1 7QX
A BPCC plc company

ISBN 0 361 079958
ISBN 0 361 07995 8 Pbk

Printed in Great Britain by
Purnell Book Production Ltd
Member of the BPCC Group

British Library Cataloguing in Publication Data

Blyton, Enid
    Brer Bear's red carrots and other
    stories.—(Brer Rabbit storybooks)
    I. Title   II. Series
    823'.912[J]   PZ7

Contents: **Page:**

Brer Bear's Red Carrots

ONCE Brer Bear had a whole field of fat red carrots. They grew there in hundreds, with their feathery green tops nodding in the breeze. Brer Rabbit thought they looked marvellous.

Now Brer Rabbit had just turned over a new leaf that week, and he felt it would be wrong to go and help himself to Brer Bear's carrots. "I must give people a chance to be kind," he said to himself. "I'll go and tell Brer Bear that I've turned over a new leaf and that I just can't let myself dig up any of his carrots without asking—and maybe he'll give me a whole lot."

So off he went to Brer Bear. Brer Bear was sitting in his front porch, basking in the sun. He wasn't very pleased to see Brer Rabbit, because he kept remembering the tricks that Brer Rabbit had played him.

"Good morning, Brer Bear," said Brer Rabbit politely. "It's a nice day, isn't it?"

"None the nicer for seeing *you*!" growled Brer Bear.

"Oh, Brer Bear! That's not a kind way to talk," said Brer Rabbit, shocked. "Why, I came to tell you that I'd turned over a new leaf!"

"About time too," said Brer Bear.

"You've a fine field of carrots," said Brer Rabbit. Brer Bear looked up at once.

"Oho! So it's my carrots you've come about," he said. "I didn't quite believe that new leaf idea of yours, Brer Rabbit."

"Well, that's just where you are wrong," said Brer Rabbit, trying to keep his temper. "I came to tell you that if I hadn't turned over a new leaf I'd have gone and dug up your carrots without asking you, to make myself some soup, but as I've made up my mind to be better in future, I came to ask you if I might have a few carrots. You can spare a few, surely?"

"Not to you Brer Rabbit, not to you," said Brer Bear. "And what's more, you can't make me give you any, no matter how many new leaves you turn over! No—once a scamp, always a scamp, is what I say, and I'm not giving any carrots to you at all."

Brer Rabbit stamped away in a rage. What was the use of turning over a new leaf if he couldn't get what he wanted? No use at all! All right—he would show Brer Bear that he would *have* to give him some carrots. Yes, he'd show him!

That night Brer Rabbit took his spade and went to Brer Bear's field. He dug up a whole sackful of fine red carrots. My, they were fat and juicy! But Brer Rabbit didn't eat a single one. No—he wasn't going to do that until Brer Bear had given him some.

He hid the sack of carrots under a bush and went home. Next morning he was up bright and early and went to the bush. He dragged the sack out and took it away down the lane not far from Brer Bear's house. It was very heavy indeed. Brer Rabbit puffed and panted as he dragged it along.

He waited until he saw Brer Bear coming down the lane for his morning walk. Then he set to work to drag the sack again, puffing as if he were a train going uphill! He pretended not to see Brer Bear, and

Brer Bear was mighty astonished to see Brer Rabbit dragging such a heavy sack down the lane.

"Heyo, Brer Rabbit," he said. "You seem to be too weak to take that sack along."

"Oh, Brer Bear, I've done such a foolish thing!" panted Brer Rabbit. "I've got such a lot of carrots to put in my store that I can't take them home! I shall have to leave them all here in the lane! Oh, why didn't you give me just a few when I asked you yesterday! Now all these will go to waste, for I'll have to leave them under a bush. I can't possibly drag the sack any farther."

Brer Bear didn't think for a moment that they could be *his* carrots. He opened the neck of the sack and looked inside. Yes, there were fine fat carrots there all right. He supposed that Brer Rabbit must have gone to market and bought them.

"You can't waste carrots," said Brer Bear. "It would be wrong."

"I know that," said Brer Rabbit. "But what am I to do?"

"I'll have them myself, if you like to take a few jars of honey in exchange for them," said Brer Bear, thinking that if he took the sackful it would save him the trouble of digging his own carrots that day.

"Oh, Brer Bear! How *kind* of you!" said Brer Rabbit, rubbing his whiskers in delight. "I thought yesterday that you were rude and unkind, Brer Bear. But today you are quite different. You are good and kind and generous. I like you."

Brer Bear couldn't help feeling pleased at this. He went into his house

and brought out three jars of honey. Brer Rabbit smelt them in delight.

"*Three* jars, Brer Bear! It's more than generous of you! How mistaken I was in you! I did so long for a few of your nice carrots yesterday, but this is almost better than carrots—though how I *do* long for carrot soup!"

"Well—you can have a few carrots out of this sackful if you like," said Brer Bear, still feeling very generous. "Here you are—one, two, three, four, five, six, seven, eight! Nice fat ones too!"

"Brer Bear, you're a mighty good friend!" said Brer Rabbit, stuffing the carrots into his big pockets and picking up the honey. "I meant to make you give me a few of your carrots—but I didn't hope that you would give me your honey too! Good-day—and thank you!"

Brer Rabbit skipped off as merry as a grasshopper in June. Brer Bear stared after him, scratching his head. Now what did Brer Rabbit mean by saying that he would *make* Brer Bear give him some of his own carrots?

And then Brer Bear suddenly had a dreadful thought and he hurried off to his field as fast as his clumsy legs would take him. There he saw where Brer Rabbit had dug up a whole sackful of carrots! And how poor Brer Bear stamped and raged!

"I've given him eight of my best carrots—and three pots of my best honey! Oh, the rascal—oh, the scamp! Turning over a leaf indeed! I'd like to turn *him* over and give him a spanking. And one of these days I will!"

But he hasn't yet! Brer Rabbit is much too clever to go near Brer Bear for a very long time.

Brer Rabbit Saves Brer Terrapin

ONE TIME Brer Fox was going down the big road and he saw old Brer Terrapin going to his home. Now Brer Fox knew Brer Terrapin was a good friend to Brer Rabbit, and it seemed to him it was a mighty good time to catch him. Brer Fox didn't have any kindly feelings towards people who were friends of Brer Rabbit.

Brer Fox ran back to his own house, which was not far off, and got a bag. Then he ran down the road again, rushed up behind Brer Terrapin, caught him up and threw him into the bag. He slung the bag across his back, then off he went, galloping home.

Brer Terrapin, he shouted, but it wasn't any good. He wriggled and struggled, but that wasn't any good either. Brer Fox just went on going, and there was old Brer Terrapin in the corner of the bag, and the bag tied up hard and fast.

But where was Brer Rabbit whilst all this was going on? Where was that long-eared, hoppetty-skippetty creature, that up-and-down-and-sailing round Brer Rabbit? He wasn't far off, you may be sure!

Brer Fox went trotting down the big road with the bag on his back—and Brer Rabbit was sitting in the bushes just by the side of the road. He saw Brer Fox trotting by and he saw the bag on his back too.

"Now what's Brer Fox got in that bag?" said Brer Rabbit to himself. "I don't know what it can be."

Well, Brer Rabbit sat in the bushes and wondered and wondered, but the more he wondered the less he could think what it was. He watched Brer Fox a-trotting down the road, and still he sat in the bushes and wondered.

"Huh!" said Brer Rabbit at last, "Brer Fox has no business to be trotting down the road carrying something other people don't know about. I guess I'll go after Brer Fox and find out what's in the bag!"

With that, Brer Rabbit set out. He hadn't got a bag to carry and he went mighty quickly. He took a short cut, and by the time Brer Fox got to his house Brer Rabbit had had time to get into his strawberry-bed and trample down a whole lot of plants. When he had done that, he sat down in some bushes where he could see Brer Fox coming home.

By and by Brer Fox came along with his bag across his back. He unlatched his door, he did, and then he threw Brer Terrapin down in a corner in the bag, and sat down to rest himself, for Brer Terrapin was mighty heavy to carry.

Brer Fox had hardly put a match to his pipe when Brer Rabbit stuck his head in at the door and shouted:

"Brer Fox! Oh, Brer Fox! You'd better take your stick and run out yonder. Coming along just now I heard a fuss going on in your garden, and I looked round and there were a whole lot of folk in your strawberry-bed, just a - trampling the strawberries down! I shouted at them, but they didn't take any notice of a little man like me. Make haste, Brer Fox, make haste! Get your stick and run. I'd go with you too, but I've got to get home. You'd better hurry, Brer Fox, if you want to save

your strawberries. Run, Brer Fox, run! Hurry now."

With that Brer Rabbit darted back into the bushes, and Brer Fox dropped his pipe and grabbed his stick and rushed out to his strawberry-bed. And no sooner was he gone than old Brer Rabbit hopped out of the bushes and into the house.

He didn't make a bit of noise. He looked round and there was the bag in the corner. He caught hold of it and felt it to see what was inside. And suddenly something yelled:

"Ow! Go away! Let me alone! Turn me loose! Ow!"

Brer Rabbit jumped back astonished. Then before you could wink an eye he slapped himself on the leg and laughed out loud.

"If I'm not making a mistake, that's nobody's voice but old Brer Terrapin's!" said Brer Rabbit.

"Is that Brer Rabbit?" yelled Brer Terrapin.

"It is," said Brer Rabbit.

"Then hurry up and get me out," said Brer Terrapin. "There's dust in my throat, grit in my eyes, and I can hardly breathe. Get me out."

"Heyo, Brer Terrapin," said Brer Rabbit. "You're a lot smarter than I am—because here you are in a bag and I don't know how in the name of goodness you've tied yourself up in there, that I don't!"

Brer Terrapin tried to explain and Brer Rabbit kept on laughing, but all the same he untied the bag, took Brer Terrapin out and carried him outside the gate. Then, when he had done this, Brer Rabbit ran off to where he knew some wasps had a nest just about as big as a football.

The wasp-nest was in a hollow tree. Brer Rabbit slipped in at the bottom of the tree and there was the nest inside. He slapped his paw over the hole where the wasps went in and out, knocked the nest down into his bag, and there he had it, wasps and all!

Then back he raced to Brer Fox's house and flung the bag down on the floor, tied up fast. Well, the way he slammed that bag down on the floor stirred all those wasps up and put them into a very bad temper! They buzzed fit to make holes in the bag!

Soon Brer Rabbit saw Brer Fox coming down the back-garden, where he had been looking for the folks that had trodden down his strawberries. He had been putting the plants straight.

By the time Brer Fox got indoors Brer Rabbit was off and away into a bush and there he sat with Brer Terrapin, waiting to see what would happen.

Brer Fox went indoors, hitting the ground with his stick, and vowing that he would shake Brer Terrapin to bits, he was in such a bad temper.

He slammed the door and Brer Rabbit and Brer Terrapin waited. They listened, but at first they couldn't hear anything. By and by they heard the most tremendous noise!

"Seems like a whole crowd of cows running round and round inside Brer Fox's house," Brer Rabbit said to Brer Terrapin.

"I can hear chairs a-falling," said Brer Terrapin.

"I can hear the table turning over," said Brer Rabbit.

"I can hear the crockery smashing," said Brer Terrapin.

"Huh!" said Brer Rabbit, enjoying himself, "Brer Fox must be having a fine game with those wasps. What a surprise he got when he opened the bag to get you—and found a wasp's nest instead!"

Just as Brer Rabbit said that, Brer Fox's door flew wide open and out rushed Brer Fox, squalling and howling as if two hundred dogs had got him by the tail!

He ran straight to the river, he did, and plunged in to get rid of the wasps on him. Brer Rabbit and Brer Terrapin sat there in the bushes and laughed and laughed, till by and by Brer Rabbit rolled over and said:

"One more laugh, Brer Terrapin, and you'll have to carry me home!"

"Get on my back then, Brer Rabbit, get on my back," said Brer Terrapin. "I'll carry you all right. Shoo! That will teach Brer Fox not to

go a-catching an old fellow like me and putting him into a dusty bag!"

Brer Fox came out of the river at last—but to this day he doesn't know how it was that though he put old Brer Terrapin into a bag, it was a nest of wasps that came out! And you may be sure Brer Rabbit never told him!

Brer Rabbit Raises the Dust

NOW ONE time it happened that Brer Fox and Brer Rabbit, Brer Wolf, Brer Bear and the rest were always up at Miss Meadows'. When Miss Meadows had chicken for dinner in would come Brer Fox and Brer Possum, and when she had fried greens in would come Brer Rabbit. If she had honey it would be Brer Bear that would come popping his head round the door.

"I can't feed everyone," said Miss Meadows to the girls. "It's getting to be a real nuisance, having all the creatures pestering round. We shall have to do something to stop them."

Well, Miss Meadows and the girls, they thought what they could do to stop the animals coming so much. And they decided that the one that could knock most dust out of a rock, he should be the one that would still come to Miss Meadows' house. The rest must stay away.

So Miss Meadows told everyone that if they would come to her house the next Saturday evening, the whole crowd of them would go down the road to where there was a big flint rock. And each of them could take up the sledge-hammer and see how much dust he could raise out of the rock.

"I shall knock out a cloud of dust!" said Brer Fox.

"You won't be able to see for miles round when I get going with that sledge-hammer!" boasted old Brer Bear.

Well, they all talked mighty biggitty except Brer Rabbit. He crept

off to a cool place and there he sat down and puzzled out how he could raise dust out of a rock. He had never seen dust got out of a rock, and he guessed he never would. But he meant to do it somehow.

By and by, whilst he was a-sitting there, up he jumped and cracked his heels together and sang out:

"Brer Buzzard is clever, and so is Brer Fox,
But Brer Rabbit makes them all pull up their socks!"

And with that he set out for Brer Racoon's house and borrowed his slippers. When Saturday night came everyone was up at Miss Meadows' house. Miss Meadows and the girls were there; and Brer Racoon, Brer Fox, Brer Wolf, Brer Bear, Brer Possum and Brer Terrapin.

Brer Rabbit shuffled up late. By the time he got to the house, everyone had gone down the road to the rock. Brer Rabbit was waiting for that—and as soon as he knew no one was at home, he crept round to the ash-bin, and filled Brer Racoon's slippers full of ashes, and then he put them on his feet and marched off!

Brer Rabbit got to the rock after a while, and as soon as Miss Meadows and the girls saw him they began to giggle and laugh because of the great big old slippers he had on.

Brer Fox laughed too, and thought of something smart to say. "I guess old Brer Rabbit's got chilblains," he said. "He's getting old."

But Brer Rabbit winked his eye at everybody and said: "You know,

folks, I've been so used to riding on horseback, as these ladies know, that I'm getting sort of tender-footed when I walk."

Then Brer Fox, he remembered how Brer Rabbit had ridden him one day, and he didn't say another word more. Everybody began to giggle, and it looked as if they would never begin hammering on the rock. Brer Rabbit picked up the sledge-hammer as if he meant to have the first try. But Brer Fox shoved Brer Rabbit out of the way and took the sledge-hammer himself.

Everyone was to have three hits at the rock with the hammer, and the one that raised the most dust out of it was the one who would be allowed to go to Miss Meadows' house as often as he liked. All the others were to keep away from the house.

Well, old Brer Fox, he grabbed the hammer, he did, and he brought it down on the rock—*blim!* No dust came. Then he drew back the hammer and down he came again on the rock—*blam!* Still no dust came. Then he spat on his hands, gave a big swing and down came the hammer—*ker-blap!* and still not a speck of dust flew!

That was Brer Fox's turn finished. Then Brer Possum had a try, but he didn't raise any dust either. After that Brer Racoon took the hammer, and tried, but he couldn't make a speck of dust come at all. Then everyone else had a try except Brer Terrapin and Brer Rabbit, but nobody raised any dust at all.

"Now it's your turn, Brer Terrapin," said Brer Fox.

But Brer Terrapin, he said no. He had watched the mighty blows the

others had given for nothing, and he wasn't going to tire himself out too.

"I've got a crick in my neck," he said. "I don't think I'll take my turn. Let Brer Rabbit have his. Looks like we'll none of us be able to raise any dust—so Miss Meadows and the girls won't have the pleasure of anybody's visit anymore!"

Brer Rabbit winked to himself, and grabbed hold of the sledge-hammer. He lifted it up into the air, and as he brought it down on the rock he jumped up and came down at the same time as the hammer—*pow!* And, of course, the ashes flew up out of his slippers and shot all round.

Brer Fox, he started sneezing away because the ashes got up his nose, and Miss Meadows and the girls began to cough and splutter.

Then Brer Rabbit lifted up the hammer again, jumped high into the air and landed with his feet and the hammer at the same time—*kerblam!*

"Stand further off, ladies!" he yelled. "Here comes the dust!"

And sure enough the dust came, for the ashes flew again out of his slippers and everyone sneezed and choked and rubbed their eyes!

Then once more Brer Rabbit jumped up and cracked his heels together and brought the hammer down on the rock–*kerblam!* "Here comes the dust!" he yelled. And sure enough, the dust came!

Well, after that there wasn't much doubt about who should be the one to visit Miss Meadows and the girls, and Brer Rabbit went off arm-in-arm with two of the girls, grinning at all the others. They stood there, blowing their noses and glaring at Brer Rabbit; and Brer Fox, he took a sneezing fit and couldn't stop till the next morning.

Brer Racoon got his slippers back from Brer Rabbit all right, and nobody ever knew what Brer Rabbit had borrowed them for. Cunning old Brer Rabbit! There wasn't much he didn't know!